Jimmy's Good deed

Bryan Roskums

Published by New Generation Publishing in 2023

Copyright © Bryan Roskums 2023

First Edition

ISBN: 978-1-80369-901-1

www.newgeneration-publishing.com

New Generation Publishing

This book is dedicated to my son Alan.

Contents

Chapter (1)

The meeting of friends.

'Mummy can I go out and play in the woods please?'

Little Jimmy Johnson called out to his Mum who was busy in the kitchen finishing drying the breakfast plates.

'Yes darling, but make sure you keep in sight of the house!—

And don't play with spiders!' She called after him.

Jimmy was eight years old and loved playing in the garden—searching for creepy crawlies, but enjoyed it most of all when he ventured into the woods and was lucky enough to catch sight of any wild animals that lived there. Today he was hoping to see more of them.

At the end of his garden was a gate that opened out to a wonderful one hundred acres of prime woodland. An area that had been fenced off sixty five years ago, trees planted to grow and develop as nature intended.

It was owned by Jimmy's Dad and was home to a variety of animals, insects, and birds.

Jimmy knew every beautiful tree and open grass space in the wood;

The trees and wild flowers had been allowed to flourish and grow, undisturbed embracing the changing seasons.

Some of the spaces had little ponds and muddy patches, so from past experience-- Jimmy knew what to wear to keep his feet dry— he went to the cupboard and pulled on his wellies without his mum having to remind him!

'Bye mum'.

Jimmy shouted as he dashed out of the back door, eager to get to the woods.

It was the month of September—autumn had crept in after the summer months, allowing the hundreds of different trees to shed their leaves, where they floated slowly down and settled gently on the forest floor creating a golden carpet.

Reaching the gate he quickly pulled the

bolt across, opened the gate and stepped into his favourite place—the woods.

Jimmy kicked the loose autumn leaves as he ran and laughed when watching the leaves as they rose in the air before floating slowly back to the ground.

Now and again he stopped running --stooped down to investigate some kind of insect activity. After a while he had reached deep into the Forest—he stood very still and listened to birds chirping above him, he loved the peace and quiet when it allowed him to hear the rustle or the sound of maybe a squirrel or a fox.

An old dead fallen tree lay stretched out behind him; walking over to it he sat down on one of its branches. He felt hot after running all that way. He gazed up at the branches of the tall trees still throwing of the last of their leaves.

It was silent all he could hear was the sound of a small sparrow singing his heart out perched on a twig just above where he was sitting.

It seemed to be looking at Jimmy—trying to get his attention.

'Hello there.'

Jimmy nearly fell of the log when he heard those words, he thought for a moment it was the bird talking to him!

'Sorry-did I frighten you?'

Jimmy gazed around him desperately trying to see who it was talking to him!

He was so shocked it took several seconds before he could find his voice, then he heard himself shout.

'Where are you, I can't see you.'

'You will if you turn round because I'm right behind you.'

The voice replied.

Jimmy quickly jumped of the old tree trunk and looked behind him, and there, squatting on a part of the old tree with a half eaten carrot in his hand was a little furry Mole.

He was dressed from head to foot in green trousers and jacket with big shiny silver buttons down the front. On his head he wore a pointed hat with a white feather sticking out from the head band.

He sat there swinging his little legs, that's

when Jimmy noticed the shoes he was wearing, made of leather with buckles that matched the buttons on his jacket.

Jimmy rubbed his eyes in disbelief it took a few seconds for him to realise he was in the woods and wasn't at home in bed—dreaming!

Cautiously he approached the log-- he edged a little closer to the little chap and spoke very slowly.

'What's your name?'

The mole stood up straight and replied.

'Well my name is Leom, and I am a mole. How do you do!'

He stretched out his tiny hand as he spoke; Jimmy looked down at him and very nervously took it between his fingers and shook it.

Because Leom was so small compared with Jimmy, as jimmy moved his fingers up and down in a handshake he sent poor Leom up in the air! Leom let out a little scream as the hand shake knocked him of off his perch—he ended up on the ground after tumberling through the long grass.

Jimmy was very upset to see what had

happened and shouted.

'Sorry Leom'

As he bent down and picked him up out of the leaves and grass onto the space beside him. Leom brushed himself down and leaned back his head—and glared at jimmy.

'You should be more careful; you could hurt somebody if you don't watch what you're doing!

Jimmy felt his face going red—just like it did when his mum told him off.

'I'm ever so sorry'. He said.

'I didn't mean to hurt you'.

Leom could see Jimmy was very embarrassed, so with a smile on his face he replied.

'Oh that's alright Jimmy—I know you didn't mean it'!

'How do you know my name Leom?'

Leom smiled

'Oh I know all about you Jimmy, I've been watching you for ages, gradually getting to know your habits and seeing how friendly you are to everyone that lives in these woods. And that's why we all think you're the one.'

Jimmy looked at the little mole with a puzzled expression on his face.

'What do you mean 'to see if I was the one?'

Leom turned round and looked left and right as if to see if anyone was listening and then he whispered.

'We badly need your help Jimmy.'

Jimmy could not understand why anyone would need his help; nobody had ever said that to him before except his mum or dad when he was asked to tidy his bedroom.

It made him feel quite important that someone else wanted his help.

Jimmy copied Leom's whisper

.'Who need's my help?'

Leom pulled out a tiny tissue from his pocket and dabbed his eyes before answering.

'I and all my friends need your help very urgently.'

'But in what way can I help you Leom?'

Leom crossed his little legs and folded his arms whilst looking Jimmy in the eye.

'Well let me explain' he squeaked'.

'Ok go ahead I'll help you if I can'.

Replied Jimmy, making himself more comfortable on the log.

Leom continued.

'All my friends and their families have lived in this wood for sixty five years, we are a very large community, we all spend time looking after this lovely place including the ants, bees, birds, and a host of other species. They all contribute in different ways to the wood that ensures every blade of grass, every tree is allowed to benefit and let nature take its course.'

Leom pushed his dapper little hat to the back of his head cleared his throat and carried on talking.

'Are you with me so far Jimmy?'

'Yes I am,' replied jimmy.

'But I still can't see how I could possibly help you?'

'Be patient son, you will soon. Now do you know who owns our wood?'

'Yes I do, my Dad owns it.'

Leom smiled,

'Very good Jimmy-- yes your Dad does own

it, but do you know he is going to sell it to a housing developer so loads of houses and roads can be built on it!'

Jimmy stood up quickly and stepped away from the log and glared at the little mole.

'No, I don't believe you Leom, You're telling me lies; my Dad would never sell this wood.'

The look on Jimmy's face was one of complete disbelief.

'Who told you that Leom; whoever it was they are not telling the truth.'

Chapter (2)

The revelation

Leom stretched out his little hand in a comforting gesture towards Jimmy.

'I'm ever so sorry Jimmy,' he said.

It was obvious to Leom that he had sprung a very hurtful surprise on his new friend; it made him feel very sad.

'I really thought you knew about it Jimmy.' He said softly.

Big tears were starting to roll down Jimmy's cheeks. It was the first time that he had heard about it, the news had affected him badly and now he wanted to go home.

'Sorry Leom, you must think I'm a big baby, but I love this wood, I come here every day to play and watch the bees and spiders, listen to the birds singing and pick flowers for my mum.

'We know- we see you.'

Jimmy wiped the tears from his eyes and looked in the direction of the sound of squeaks and barking sounds coming from somewhere amongst the trees.

'Where's that noise coming from.' He asked.

'That my friend is coming from all our pals gathered together waiting to hear some good news.'

Leom stood up and made himself look bigger by stretching his tiny arms above his head.

'Come with me my friend and I will take you to meet them, after which you will know how you can help us and at the same time yourself.'

'Well yes—alright I would like that Leom, but I still can't see how I can help you.'

'Follow me and you will find out'.

Jimmy fell in behind Leom as he set off into the thickest part of the wood and was very surprised at the speed he was travelling.

In and out of the thick undergrowth between the trees and over the ditches he went-- when suddenly Leom came to an abrupt stop.

Jimmy watched as he knocked on a tiny front door, after one minute the door opened and there a tiny mouse popped his head out, when he saw Leom standing outside his door, he said in a squeaky voice.

'Oh no, not you Leom, you always bring trouble when you knock on my door!'

But he was laughing when he said it so Jimmy knew he was only joking.

The little mouse stepped out on to the grass and gave Leom a hug and said.

'What's new my friend?'

'Well I think I have some good news for you, but to hear what it is you'll have to come to the usual meeting place and bring as many friends you meet along the way. Oh and I would like you to meet my new friend Jimmy.'

On hearing that Jimmy stepped forward and very politely said.

'Good afternoon er, er,' Jimmy started to stutter.

'I'm sorry I didn't get your name'?

'Well I can understand that because I didn't tell you my name lad-but I will tell you now.'

The little mouse stood up on his hind legs trying to make himself taller.

'My name' he said giving a small bow.

'Is Archibald truelove and I'm very pleased to meet you Jimmy.'

'And I'm very pleased to meet you too.'

Jimmy replied with a little smile.

'Ok that's enough chit chat from you too, we've got a very important meeting to go to.' Shouted Leom.

'Come on young Jimmy follow me--see you at the meeting Archie-don't be late!

Another five minutes and after Pushing their way through the bushes and climbing a small incline they emerged in to a large clearing

Jimmy stopped in his tracks when he saw what was in front of him, bringing his hands quickly up to cover his eyes, he didn't believe what he saw. Slowly he moved his fingers apart to create a gap and peeked through them, he was both excited and amazed when the chattering suddenly went silent. He drew in a deep breath as he took in the scene before him.

Creatures of all descriptions had formed

a circle- some of them perched up in the surrounding trees, all of them staring at him.

He started to go red in the face, feeling a bit embarrassed, he quickly pulled himself together and stared back at them.

There were rabbits, foxes, badgers, hedgehogs, squirrels and all kinds of birds all sitting quietly until Leom stepped forward and raised his arms in the air.

It was then they all began to cheer and call out his name, Leom kept waving his arms and shouting out for quiet as he tried to reach above the noise his friends were making but not having much success. The excited throng were not taking any notice of little Leom's efforts.

Jimmy was feeling sad for Leom, he felt he couldn't just stand there doing nothing so he lifted his arms and shouted at the top of his voice

'STOP! '

It came out loud and clear and even surprised Jimmy.

His voice rose above the din; it suddenly went quiet, as if he had just turned off a water tap.

'Please let Leom speak to you'. He cried.

Jimmy was so surprised how much his intervention had had on all the little creatures his face started to go red again, making him feel he wanted to hide away. Now they were all looking at him which made it worse.

'Who are you'?

The voice sounded as if it came from the back. Jimmy stood on tip toe to try and see who it was and the same squeaky voice shouted.

'You don't have to get any taller to see me mate, look up-I'm in the tree above you!

Jimmy quickly bent his head back and there perched on a twig was a rather large, scruffy looking blackbird.

They stared at each other for about ten seconds, and then fed up waiting for an answer; the bird stretched his scrawny neck and croaked.

'Lost your tongue boy?' tell us your name laddie?'

Leom jumped in front of Jimmy.

'Don't let him talk to you like that'.

Then glaring up at the blackbird he said.

'Scrummy this is my friend- his name is

Jimmy- he is going to try to save our woods so treat him with the utmost respect!'

'Alright.' replied scrummy.

'Sorry Leom, I was out of order. Hello Jimmy- my name is Scrummy, how are you going to help us then?'

'HI Scrummy', acknowledged Jimmy.

'I am going to try and persuade my Dad not to sell our woods.' answering with a bit more confidence.

Scrummy gave out a loud squawk, raised his head as high as he could and flapped his wings.

'That's wonderful young Jimmy sir,' he screeched.

'If you can do that you will save all our lives!'

'Yes',

Interrupted Leom as he turned to face the meeting, gathered in front of him.

'You are all aware by now that Jimmy's Dad intends to sell our woods to a builder so houses can be built on it-- our friend Jimmy is going to try and stop it happening'.

Turning to face Jimmy he said.

'That's right isn't it?'

'Yes'. He replied.

'I'm certainly going to do my best for us all because don't forget this place means as much to me as it does you!'

Before he could utter another word another voice entered the debate.

'Just a minute there'.

The tone had authority running through it. Every one's eyes were drawn to and focused on a spot where a hole in the bark of big oak tree was the home of a big old barn owl.

He was now perched on a broken branch just outside his front door. Shaking his feathered head he gazed down and looked over at the crowd.

'Now I have been listening to what's going on and I get the gist of it.'

Turning his attention towards Jimmy

'Hello young lad, my name is Winger(Fly by night) Roundhead, I've got more brains than all this lot put together and I can tell you now we have an uphill fight on our hands!

If we want to stand any chance of winning this battle we must have a plan. What have you got to say about that Young sir?'

'Hello Winger',-replied Jimmy.

'It sounds like a good idea to me but I don't know how to make a plan?'

Winger stretched his black wings out as far as they would go and leaned forward so much -Jimmy thought he was going to fall of his perch!

'You don't have to make a plan laddie, we will make it for you and you will make it work for us--with our help of course.'

Winger looked down at all his friends who were hanging on to every word he uttered.

'Do you all agree he bellowed?'

There was an almighty roar of approval from the crowd.

'Yeeeeeees',.

They were jumping in the air with joy, whistling, and dancing with each other.

Archibald Truelove was sitting on the top of Winger's front door when he squeaked.

'Alright, alright, calm down everybody, nothing's happened yet-don't get too exited.'

'That's good advice Archie.'

Broke in Winger.

'One of the first things we have to do is to form a working team made up from volunteers.

'I would like to be in the team.'

Called out a fox that was up on his hind legs at the Back, trying his best to get recognition.

I and my family have lived in these woods as long as I can remember so I will do anything to save the wood.'

'What's your name my friend? Asked Winger'

'My name is Crafty F. Fothrington, I and my partner have two cubs.'

'Alright Crafty, consider yourself on the team.'

'I would also like to join the team-my name is Chipper Badger, I too have a family.'

'You also are accepted Chipper.'

Said Winger.

'Now anyone else that feels they can contribute to the cause, I think we should meet up again tomorrow at ten o'clock.'

A big brown rat was standing quite close to Jimmy when he said.

'I think that I would be an asset to the team, but should we not vote for a leader first, by the way my name is Ratty Bystander.'

Jimmy interrupted, holding his hand in the air.

'Can I say something?' He cried.

'We are all ear's'

Shouted Scrummy through his laughter.

'Yes carry on laddie-What is it?' Queried Winger.

'Well Winger, I think you should be the leader!'

'And what, dear boy, guide's you to that conclusion?'

Jimmy was ready with his answer.

'Because my Dad say's Owl's are very wise old birds'.

'Well I don't know about the old bit, but I think I would like your Dad

He must be very wise himself. And thank you Jimmy for your vote of confidence.

'This must be done properly with a vote, do you all agree?'

There was a hush that seemed to settle around

everyone after Winger had finish speaking, it lasted for about thirty seconds and then what started as a faint murmuring and a muttering of voices suddenly erupted into a crowd all trying to talk at once. Then someone shouted.

'Leader, leader, leader. '

Everyone gradually joined in with.

'Winger is our leader, Winger is our leader.'

'Ok I get the message loud and clear' said Winger

Trying to make himself heard over the noise.

'If that's what everyone wants-then so be it-I'll be your leader.

'But I am going to need some help my friends, I know a lot of you have families to look after so you will be excused, also for those of you that usually work at night won't be needed.

So anyone else that would like to volunteer-we'll meet here tomorrow at ten O'clock-now all go home. Goodbye!'

Jimmy and Leom stood looking at each other for a few seconds.

'Well said Leom that ended abruptly.'

'Yes.' replied Jimmy.

'But at least we've made a start! Any way Leom I'm going home now I'll see you tomorrow.'

Leom looked a little tired as he said.

'Ok Jimmy, I'm going to bed.'

Chapter (3)

Mission Impossible.

Jimmy awoke to the sound of music drifting up from somewhere down stairs, he felt excited, as the events of yesterday began to flood his memory. Jumping out of bed he ran into the bathroom, showered and brushed his teeth-still preoccupied with his friends in the woods.

Sat at the table tucking into egg on toast he glanced at his Dad who sat next to him reading the morning newspaper. Jimmy was absorbed with ways of bringing up the subject of the woods. He knew what to say, that was not the problem, the problem as far as he was concerned was getting the right opportunity.

His mum suddenly called out from the kitchen.

'Tommy (that was his Dad's name) would you like another cup of tea?'

Tommy put the paper down on to the table and replied.

'Yes please my dear.'

Jimmy seized the chance.

'Dad can I ask you a question?'

'Of course you can son.' he replied.

'What is it you want to know?'

Jimmy thought he would be better off if he was standing up.

Getting out of his chair, he stood in front of his Dad.

Come on then son what is it? Prompted his Dad softly.

Jimmy took a couple of deep breaths.

'Well Dad.' He stumbled.

His Dad laughed.

'Jimmy It can't be that bad!

'Are you going to sell the wood?

The words tumbled out of his mouth before he had time to think about it.

His Dad looked a bit shocked'

'Well—yes Jimmy- there's going to be

houses built on the land, why did you want to know that?'

'Because if you sell it I'll have nowhere to play with my friends!'

Tommy looked across at his wife who was handing him a mug of tea; he took it with a puzzled expression on his face.

Turning towards Jimmy he questioned.

'I didn't know you played with your friends in the wood? How can you play football in the woods?'

'No I don't mean the friends I play football with! These are my other friends, they all live in the wood and have families that help each other and work hard to help the wood grow.'

'Jimmy, if there are people living in our wood without permission they must be travellers and travellers are not welcome in there.'

Tommy turned towards his wife.

'Did you know anything about this Julie?'

'Well no I didn't, it's the first time I've heard about people living in the wood. I'm afraid Daddy's right darling, people cannot live in the wood!'

Jimmy just sat there looking at his mum, after a small silence he said.

'Mum I have never seen people living in the wood.'

His mum suddenly got up from her chair and stood back from the table.

Jimmy you have just told us you play with your friends in the wood, and now you're saying you've never seen any people in there, which is it?'

Jimmy was becoming a little impatient.

'Mum I do play with my friends in the woods, but they are not people, they are all different kinds of animals and birds- they are my friends!'

Both his parents started to laugh but stopped when they saw the look on Jimmy's face, they could see he was embarrassed.'

'You had us running around in circles for a while son. 'Exclaimed his Dad.

Jimmy looked down at his hands as he spoke.

'Sorry Mum, sorry Dad, It's my fault.'

His mum sat next to him and gave him a little hug as she whispered in his ear.

'It was no one's fault darling, just a little misunderstanding.'

'Yes', agreed Tommy.

'We all got a bit mixed up there didn't we son, now we've sorted that out. Let's get back to your original question. Yes we are thinking of selling the land-we don't use it for anything other than going for a walk now and again when the weather's nice.'

'But Dad, I use it all the time.' Interrupted Jimmy.

'I use it all the time, I love it, I've made friends with lots of animals, and I know all the birds that come there too.'

Tommy smiled at his son.

'Look, your mum and I are very pleased that you enjoy going into the woods and all the wild life in there, but It's sad to say they will have to find somewhere else to live.'

Jimmy felt he was losing the battle.

'But Dad there is nowhere around here they could move to, they and their past family's have lived in the woods for a long long time looking after it.'

'yes Jimmy I do understand what you are saying, your Mum and I appreciate how much the woods mean to you personally, but now you're getting older you have got to start learning how you look at situations from both sides. If you do that, then you are able to make an informed decision.'

Jimmy sat looking at his Dad for a few seconds before he spoke.

'Well I've told you my side, now tell me the other side.'

Tommy and Julie looked at each other completely lost for words.

Then Julie took hold of Jimmy's hands and pulled him close to her.

'Let me try and explain.' She said.

'There are thousands of people looking for somewhere to live-like young families who would like to have more children but because it would mean moving to a bigger house they sometimes have to wait till the right house comes on the market. So that means there must be a constant stream of new builds for sale!'

The only way that can happen is for land like

ours to be made available for the builders. Do you understand what I'm saying Jimmy?'

'Yes Mum, of course I understand all that you've told me. But all the animals that live in the wood are just as important to us- my teacher at school say's without them people would not survive! Is that true?'

Tommy leaned forward in his chair as he spoke.

'Yes my boy, your teacher is correct, we do need all of nature to exist, but sometimes it's a simple question of priorities and in this case I think the building of houses comes top! Which means the woods will be sold-I'm sorry son but there it is?'

Jimmy got up slowly from the table, looked at his parents and said.

'Ok Dad-Mum I'm going in the woods now, is that ok?'

'Yes.'

But only for a couple of hours darling.' said Julie.

As Jimmy stepped into the woods he glanced at his watch, it read nine forty five, and the meeting was at ten o'clock so he was in good time.

As he passed Archie's front door, Archie was just coming out.

'Good Morning Jimmy.'

'Good morning Archie.'

Was the reply.

' lovely day, looking forward to the meeting?'

'Yes and no,'

'What do you mean by that?' asked Jimmy.

The little mouse tweaked his whiskers before replying.

'Well of course I always look forward to meeting up with my friends, but to be honest, on this occasion I think It will be a waste of time'

'Please don't say that Archie, especially in front of the other team members!'

'Why not? I thought that was the purpose of the team.' said Archie. 'Airing all our opinions?'

'Yes of course, you're quite right.'

Another five minutes and they had reached the meeting place without another word between them.

Winger, scrummy, Leom, and Chipper were already in attendance, we are just waiting for Ratty Bystander and Crafty Fothrington, and then we can start said Winger. As he spoke they both arrived and settled with the other members of the team in a circle.

Winger began by thanking all for coming.

'You all are very aware why we are having this meeting, we all need to contribute to the discussion, and I'm sure you know how important the final decision whether the wood is sold or not will be, without sounding too dramatic, a matter of life and death for some of us!'

Winger stretched, as if to exercise his wings.

'I'm going to ask our friend Jimmy to start.'

Jimmy spent some time in explaining what had transpired between his Mother, father, and himself.

Scrummy started screeching.

'What's the point of discussing this any longer, it sounds as if Jimmy's Dad has made up his mind about selling the wood.'

Leom spoke up.

'If that's all you can come up with Scrummy, you might as well go back home, we need to be positive and come up with good idea's'

'Hang on Leom, Scrums' got a point.'

Intervened Chipper.

'We are all facing a national emergency and therefore unless we are willing to take extreme measures in order to get a positive result,

Then yes, we are up the creek etc!'

'Ok' said Winger.

'It's obvious to me your all very passionate regarding the ultimate outcome, so I think we should consider Chipper's suggestion of looking at extreme measures to get Jimmy's Dad to change his mind.'

Ratty raised his hand seeking permission to speak.

'Yes.' Queried Winger.

'Well, I think we should try and recruit the kids at Jimmy's school.'

'How the devil are we expected to do that?' Screeched scrummy.

'What and how would they be able to help us if we did recruit them?'

Leom joined in the discussion.

'There is one thing the kids could do.'

'Yes what's that? Said Crafty.

'They could stick posters all over town and bring it to the notice of the public!'

'Yes and I know another way that might change his mind.'

Said Archie, scratching away at his neck.

'We could all invade jimmy's house, I'm sure his Dad would

Not appreciate us lot trampling around inside his lovely home?'

Winger called everyone to order.

'I think we have made considerable progress today, now I think it's time to close this meeting and for all of you to spread the update to the rest of our friends to get their opinions. We'll meet again next Sunday at the same time.'

Chapter (4)

Where there's a will!

Jimmy's Dad was outside in the back garden cutting the grass when he arrived home.

'Hello son.' He greeted.

'Have you been enjoying yourself?'

'Yes Dad' I've seen all my friends and they are not very happy with you.'

Tommy stopped the mower.

'And why are your friends not happy with me.'

'Because you're selling the wood of course' replied Jimmy.

'Oh not that again son, I thought we'd settled that this morning.'

Jimmy looked at his Dad and said.

'Not by a long way Dad, not by a long way.'

He walked into the house and called out.

'I'm home Mum'.

His Mother looked up from the book she was reading.

'Hello darling, did you have a nice time with your friends?'

'Yes Mum, they are all very worried.'

'What are they worried about Jimmy?'

'Losing their place where they live of course!'

Julie slotted the bookmarker between the pages of her book and placed it on the table.

'Come and sit down Jimmy.'

She coaxed, patting the seat next to her.'

'I think we should have a talk.'

Without speaking he sat down and snuggled up close to her.

'I know what you want to talk to me about Mum.' He started.

'It's about the wood?'

'Yes Jimmy, I want to know how you worked out the animals or your friends as you call them were worried? They certainly can't talk!'

Jimmy was looking down at his hands, desperately trying to think of an explanation that would sound plausible.

Mum I have grown very close to the birds, foxes, badgers and many more animals they come up to me and take food from my hands because they know they can trust me. That's how I know they are concerned about Dad's decision to get rid of the woods. When I look at them--at their eyes, they look so sad.'

' Oh dear Jimmy you shouldn't be concerning yourself with matter's like this, your too young and sensitive, you should be out playing football instead of spending so much time in that wood!'

'Your Dad's made up his mind about it now son, so please let it rest, if you keep on about it you'll put your Dad in a bad mood.'

'Fair enough Mum.'

But Jimmy had no intention of letting it rest, already he was beginning to form a counter attack, he knew there was a way of saving the woods.

Christmas had come and gone, there was a feeling of spring in the air, and Birds were busy building and rebuilding their nests.

Snakes, wood frogs, and other animals were waking up from hibernation.

Daffodils were showing off their yellow bell like faces spreading their colour across the forest floor.

But there was something else going on in the wood that didn't match the joy of spring,

The animals and all other forms of life that lived in the woods were going about their business as usual, but they all looked very sad!

That was because the passing of time and all sorts of tactics during the winter months had not altered Tommy's mind, in fact he had started negotiations with several potential customers about plans for the future of the land.

Jimmy sat at the breakfast table with his Mum and Dad on a beautiful sunny day, it was mid April and a meeting was due to be held at the usual venue this very morning.

Jimmy glanced at his watch; he still had two hours before he needed to leave.

He had, over the last couple of months, bought the subject of the pending sale up with his parents.

His mother and father seemed to have lost interest in discussing it with him anymore.

Chapter (5)

Unanimous Decision

Jimmy arrived at the meeting in good time as usual; all the other members of the team with the exception of Crafty Fothrington (who had been missing for weeks) were there.

Winger spoke in a low tone, as though he didn't want to be there.

Friends, he said, I feel as though we have explored every avenue we can come up with regarding our home.

We've exhausted every possible opportunity that has presented itself over the last twelve months-all to no avail.

So it is with great regret that I have to say I will be resigning at the end of this meeting.

'You can't do that.'

Shouted Leom.

'You promised you would be our leader and leaders do not quit!'

Scrummy stretched his legs and flapped his wings, which caused a black shadow to envelope the meeting.

'Not so fast winger, there are other ways this can be tackled, ways that we haven't even thought about.'

Winger responded.

'Then why have you not bought them to the table before?'

Because Winger.

I've only just found out myself!'

Chipper piped up with.

'Then Perhaps you wouldn't mind letting us into the secrete Scrum?'

'Yes and I'll ignore the sarcastic remark Chipper. I was flying over the town yesterday, covering most of it, I noticed in my travels the lack of leisure parks there is. Places where humans can walk and maybe have picnics in the sun shine.'

'Well I'm glad you enjoyed your outing

Scrummy but what has humans having picnics got to do with us?'

Winger was the first to realise where Scrummy was going with his Idea.

'Brilliant!' Scrummy, absolutely brilliant, I think I know what you're about to share with us. So carry on.'

'Thanks' replied Scummy.

'Well first of all I came to this conclusion because I was searching for places that were similar to these woods and when I finished and could not find anywhere. It came to me that if we had nowhere to move to, humans had nowhere to walk their dogs and enjoy picnics under the trees.' This place is fenced of keeping the humans out, but what if the fence was taken down? We could share the woods!'

Jimmy answered.

'Yes scrummy that's a good idea but it's not going to stop my Dad selling this wood.'

Ratty who up to now had given the impression he was sound asleep, suddenly popped his head up and said.

'Well I think we are on to something that

with a bit of research could lead us with the result we have been searching for.'

'Ok.' cut in Winger.

'I think Scrummy might have found a potential solution. What he means is cutting the woods in half, one half to build the houses and one half for the humans to enjoy, and also giving us a place to live!

Everyone was happy with that assessment.

It was agreed that Jimmy would approach his Father about the Idea and report back to the team.

Chapter (6)

New beginnings

Jimmy was sitting beside his mother in the lounge the day after the meeting. His Dad was away on business for a couple of days.

Jimmy was thinking to himself this might be a good time to broach the subject of the pending wood sale, while his Dad was away.

His mother was reading and looked relaxed, which made him think without his Dad there, she just might be a little more receptive to the new Idea!

'Mum, can I talk to you about the woods?'

His Mum put down the book she had been reading.

'Of course you can sweetie, but you don't have to ask, I'm always available to talk to you.'

She gave him a little hug and kissed his forehead.

'So what do you want to talk about?'

Jimmy explained what the new Idea was—splitting the land.

A percentage of the woods to be handed to the local authority, so it can be developed into a public park—and the remainder made available to the developers for building new homes.

'You see Mum, the people would have a nice green space to play and walk in-- the builders would be able to build their houses—and I would still be able to play with my friends!

Julie was looking at her son, somewhat shaken, having a hard time believing those words had just came out of his mouth.

'Where did you get all that from?'

She asked with a shocked surprise on her face.

Jimmy knew he couldn't tell his mum the truth--how he came upon this solution-- about the regular meetings with his friends in the wood. He didn't like telling lies—he knew his

Mum and Dad would be very angry if they ever found out he was lying.

But on this occasion he felt it would be justifiable.

'Mum, I told a lot of my friends at school about the sale of the wood, and also one of my teachers—and it's what they came up with!'

'Well, I must say-I think they might have discovered the solution to the problem. I agree with all you've told me Jimmy and I'm going to try and persuade your Father to agree to it.'

Jimmy leapt of his seat and jumped for joy, at the same time letting out a scream at the top of his voice.

'Oh thank you Mum—do you think Dad will go for it?'

Julie stood up and cuddled her son.

'Yes--I really think he will darling.'

Tommy arrived back home the next day— Julie wasted no time in telling him about the new plan—Tommy noticed she was quite excited about it.

'Yes Julie – I think that plan would suite every one. The people would love somewhere to walk their dogs—and also the children would have a safe place to play!'

The following week Tommy had negotiated the terms for the sale of sixty percent of the land with a well known house builder.

The local council had agreed to accept the gift of the remaining forty percent and to make available the funds to turn it into a public Park, including a children's play ground.

It was a beautiful Saturday Morning; Tommy was playing football with Jimmy in their back garden, the sun was providing a warm glow over the whole area—a gentle breeze rustled the newly formed leaves on the branches of the trees above them.

Their concentration was suddenly interrupted when—a loud repeating squawk above them broke the silence. Caw, caw, caw.

Jimmy recognised the sound immediately— he looked up and there—with wide spread wings—gliding effortlessly round in circles— was Scrummy the Blackbird.

The loud squawk also drew Tommy's eyes skyward --he noticed the bird was moving its head from side to side as though looking for something.

But Jimmy knew that Scrummy was sending him a message—he was asking Jimmy to come to the meeting place a.s.a.p.

Tommy looked at his son and pointed upwards.

'He's making a lot of noise over something; I think I've seen that bird before.'

'Yes dad, so have I—he makes a lot of noise but he's friendly.'

Julie called out from the house that lunch was ready, ending the football session. That was good timing thought Jimmy as he gave thumbs up to Scrummy on his way in to the house.

Chapter (7)

The lesson of life

Jimmy finished his lunch and with his parent's permission-- made his way into the woods. He could see Scrummy above him going to the same place; someone has called a meeting he thought?

He heard the chattering well before he arrived at the usual meeting place, when he got there most of the same crowd were in attendance.

His friend Leom was missing also two of the rabbits that were usually at the meetings.

Winger was perched up in his usual place just outside his front door, spreading his wings he called for order.

After waiting patiently for the noise to abate he nestled them back to his side and said.

'Friends I have called this meeting today because of the importance of the changes we all will be facing very shortly.

'You have been informed of the decision Jimmy's Dad has made-- to compromise and split our woods into two sections.

Which means of course we will all move and settle in one half, I understand that will be near to where Jimmy lives.'

Winger was interrupted when everyone started clapping and cheering.

'Calm down' said Winger.

'You'll still see plenty of him, He won't change his habits.'

'Your right Winger.' Shouted Jimmy.

'Everything will be the same for me!'

Winger continued.

'You must pay respects to your friends that have lived there all their lives—but there is plenty of room for everyone there so there will not be a problem.'

'Before I close this meeting—I would like to thank Jimmy on behalf of myself and everyone here—and for our recently departed friends, without whose help—make no mistake, we would have ended up homeless.

I would also like to thank all of you predators who promised to restrain from hunting down our friends that served on the team—they all survived with the exception of just three.

One more favour I ask of you, please when this meeting closes, allow ten minutes before you start hunting for your dinner!

I'll say good bye and good luck to you all. This meeting is closed!'

Jimmy felt very sad, it had suddenly occurred to him why Leom and the two rabbits weren't there at the meeting.

He wasted no time in heading for home stopping briefly next to the log where he first met Leom—and remembered him.

The following months saw big changes to the woods, drains were laid, electricity and gas, were connected to the land roads were built very quickly. And a lot of trees were cut down.

Two, three and four bedroom houses started to appear as if by magic.

Jimmy continued with his regular jaunts into

the woods, but now the gate at the bottom of his garden was no longer there. He had to go through the brand knew golden painted gates the entrance to the new public park.

Three years after Leom first informed Jimmy; his Dad intended to sell the woods, Tommy, Julie and Jimmy passed through the gates and entered the park for the first time.

The first thing they noticed was a metal fenced off area, which made them smile. It was a children's playground,

Full of little kids—on swings, roundabouts, slides and tunnels, all laughing and having a wonderful time!

Jimmy stopped walking- stood where he was for a couple of minutes and took in all the activity going on around him which made him feel overjoyed.

Catching up with his parents- Jimmy tugged on his Dad's jacket and pointed.

'Look what you've done Dad! Look what you've done, are you pleased Dad?

Tommy stopped walking, put both arms around his son and whispered. Thank you

Jimmy, you are a wonderful boy, if it hadn't been for you and your mother those tots would not be enjoying themselves with their Mum's and Dad's in this lovely Park!'

'Also Dad all the creatures have somewhere permanent to live happily for the next hundred years.

THE END